The Caper of the Crown Jewels: GREAT BRITAIN

Join Secret Agent Jack Stalwart

on his other adventures:

The Search for the Sunken Treasure: **AUSTRALIA**

The Secret of the Sacred Temple: **CAMBODIA**

The Mystery of the Mona Lisa: **FRANCE**

The Pursuit of the Ivory Poachers: **KENYA**

The Escape of the Deadly Dinosaur: **USA**

The Caper of the Crown Jewels: GREAT BRITAIN

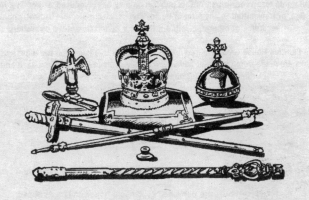

Elizabeth Singer Hunt

Illustrated by Brian Williamson

RED FOX

THE CAPER OF THE CROWN JEWELS: GREAT BRITAIN
A RED FOX BOOK 978 1 862 30474 1

First published in Great Britain by Chubby Cheeks Publications Limited
Published in this edition by Red Fox,
an imprint of Random House Children's Books

Chubby Cheeks edition published 2005
This edition published 2007

The Random House Group Limited makes every effort to ensure that the papers used in its
books are made from trees that have been legally sourced from well-managed and credibly
certified forests. Our paper procurement policy can be found at:
www.randomhouse.co.uk/paper.htm

Mixed Sources
Product group from well-managed
forests and other controlled sources
www.fsc.org Cert no. TT-COC-2139
© 1996 Forest Stewardship Council

Set in Meta, Trixie, American Typewriter, Luggagetag, Gill Sans Condensed and Serpentine.

Red Fox Books are published by Random House Children's Books,
61–63 Uxbridge Road, London W5 5SA.
A Random House Group Company

www.**kids**at**randomhouse**.co.uk

Addresses for companies within The Random House Group Limited can be found at:
www.randomhouse.co.uk/offices.htm

THE RANDOM HOUSE GROUP Limited Reg. No. 954009

A CIP catalogue record for this book is available from the British Library.

Printed and bound in Great Britain by Cox & Wyman Ltd, Reading, Berkshire

*For the children who supported
Jack and me in the early days*

Destination:
GREAT BRITAIN

JACK STALWART

Jack Stalwart applied to be a secret
agent for the Global Protection
Force four months ago.

My name is Jack Stalwart. My older brother,
Max, was a secret agent for you, until he
disappeared on one of your missions. Now I
want to be a secret agent too. If you choose
me, I will be an excellent secret agent and get
rid of evil villains, just like my brother did.

Sincerely,

Jack Stalwart

HIGHLY CONFIDENTIAL

Jack Stalwart was sworn in as a Global
Protection Force secret agent four months ago.
Since that time, he has completed all of his
missions successfully and has stopped no less
than twelve evil villains. Because of this he
has been assigned the code name 'COURAGE'.

Jack has yet to uncover the whereabouts of
his brother, Max, who is still working for this
organization at a secret location. Do not give
Secret Agent Jack Stalwart this information.
He is never to know about his brother.

Gerald Barter
Director, Global Protection Force

THINGS YOU'LL FIND IN EVERY BOOK

Watch Phone: The only gadget Jack wears all the time, even when he's not on official business. His Watch Phone is the central gadget that makes most others work. There are lots of important features, most importantly the 'C' button, which reveals the code of the day – necessary to unlock Jack's Secret Agent Book Bag. There are buttons on both sides, one of which ejects his life-saving Melting Ink Pen. Beyond these functions, it also works as a phone and, of course, gives Jack the time of day.

Global Protection Force (GPF): The GPF is the organization Jack works for. It's a worldwide force of young secret agents whose aim is to protect the world's people, places and possessions. No one knows exactly where its main offices are located (all correspondence and gadgets for repair are sent to a special PO Box, and training is held at various locations around the world), but Jack thinks it's somewhere cold, like the Arctic Circle.

Whizzy: Jack's magical miniature globe. Almost every night at precisely 7:30 p.m., the GPF uses Whizzy to send Jack the identity of the country that he must travel to. Whizzy can't talk, but he can cough up messages. Jack's parents don't know Whizzy is anything more than a normal globe.

The Magic Map: The magical map hanging on Jack's bedroom wall. Unlike most maps, the GPF's map is made of a mysterious wood. Once Jack inserts the country piece from Whizzy, the map swallows Jack whole and sends him away on his missions. When he returns, he arrives precisely one minute after he left.

Secret Agent Book Bag: The Book Bag that Jack wears on every adventure. Licensed only to GPF secret agents, it contains top-secret gadgets necessary to foil bad guys and escape certain death. To activate the bag before each mission, Jack must punch in a secret code given to him by his Watch Phone. Once he's away, all he has to do is place his finger on the zip, which identifies him as the owner of the bag and immediately opens.

THE STALWART FAMILY

Jack's dad, John

He moved the family to England when Jack was two, in order to take a job with an aerospace company. As far as Jack knows, his dad designs and manufactures aeroplane parts. Jack's dad thinks he is an ordinary boy and that his other son, Max, attends a school in Switzerland. Jack's dad is American and his mum is British, which makes Jack a bit of both.

Jack's mum, Corinne

One of the greatest mums as far as Jack is concerned. When she and her husband received a letter from a posh school in Switzerland inviting Max to attend, they were overjoyed. Since Max left six months ago, they have received numerous notes in Max's handwriting telling them he's OK. Little do they know it's all a lie and that it's the GPF sending those letters.

Jack's older brother, Max

Two years ago, at the age of nine, Max joined the GPF. Max used to tell Jack about his adventures and show him how to work his secret-agent gadgets. When the family received a letter inviting Max to attend a school in Europe, Jack figured it was to do with the GPF. Max told him he was right, but that he couldn't tell Jack anything about why he was going away.

Nine-year-old Jack Stalwart

Four months ago, Jack received an anonymous note saying: 'Your brother is in danger. Only you can save him.' As soon as he could, Jack applied to be a secret agent too. Since that time, he's battled some of the world's most dangerous villains, and hopes some day in his travels to find and rescue his brother, Max.

DESTINATION:
Great Britain

Great Britain is made up of three countries: England, Scotland and Wales

•

Its capital city, London, is one of the most famous cities in the world

•

Big Ben, Westminster Abbey, the Houses of Parliament, the London Eye, Buckingham Palace and the Tower of London are located there

•

The two 'houses' of Parliament, the House of Commons and the House of Lords, have been around since the Middle Ages

The London 'Eye' is actually an enormous Ferris wheel located next to the River Thames

•

Queen Elizabeth II is one of the longest reigning monarchs in British history. She has ruled for over fifty years

•

The Queen's jewels – the Crown Jewels – are housed in the Tower of London

THE TOWER OF LONDON: A HISTORY

The Tower of London has been the home and fortress of the British monarchy for nearly 900 years

It's not one tower, but a series of towers, buildings, walled walks and lawns

Throughout history, the Tower has been used as a treasury, zoo, prison and weapons storehouse

Prisoners arrived at the Tower by boating down the River Thames and passing underneath Traitors' Gate

Today, the Tower serves as a tourist attraction where people can learn about its history and see the Queen's Crown Jewels

THE CROWN JEWELS:
Facts and Figures

The Crown Jewels is the name given to the ceremonial crowns, orbs, sceptres (pronounced *sep-ters*), plates, spoons, rings and clothing used by the British monarchy

♦

Many of the pieces were made in the 1600s during the reign of Charles II

♦

Except for three swords and a spoon, all regalia made before the reign of Charles II was destroyed in 1649 at Oliver Cromwell's command

The largest cut diamond in the world, the Cullinan I, sits on top of the Sovereign's Sceptre with Cross. It weighs 530 carats

♦

Queen Elizabeth II wears the Imperial State Crown at the opening of Parliament. It was made in 1937

♦

Since the fourteenth century, the Crown Jewels have been kept at the Tower of London. During the Second World War, they were moved to a secret hiding place

THE YEOMAN WARDER

Yeoman Warders are also known as 'Beefeaters'

Their legendary life at the Tower began more than 500 years ago. They were responsible for guarding the Tower of London and its prisoners

Today, their role is the same, although they don't watch over prisoners any more. Instead, they give guided tours on the Tower's history

One of the Yeoman Warders, the Ravenmaster, takes care of the Tower's black birds. Legend has it that if the ravens leave, the monarchy will fall

MAGIC FINGERS

You will need:
A cup of water
Black pepper
A bar of soap

Before the trick:
Rub the bar of soap
over one of your fingers.

The trick:
Take the cup of water and sprinkle lots of black pepper on the top. Ask for a volunteer to dip their finger in and try to push the pepper away; it will only stick to their fingers.

Then tell them you've got magic fingers. Lean over the cup, wiggle your fingers and say 'Presto Pepper!' Slowly lower the finger with soap on it into the water and watch as the pepper magically separates!

DISAPPEARING COIN

You will need:
2 sheets of coloured paper
A clear glass
A coin
A handkerchief
A wand or pencil
Clear sticky tape

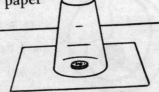

Before the trick:
Turn the glass upside down onto the first piece of coloured paper. Trace the rim and cut the circle out. Then tape it to the mouth of the glass, trying to make the tape invisible.

The trick:
Put the other sheet of paper on a table with the coin and upside-down glass next to each other. Tell everyone that you're going to make the coin disappear. Place the handkerchief over the glass. Carefully lift and slide the glass on top of the coin and tap it with the wand. Say 'Abracadabra!' and lift the handkerchief. The coin's disappeared!

SECRET AGENT GADGET INSTRUCTION MANUAL

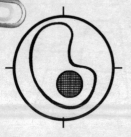 **Ear Amp:** When you need to listen in on some crooks or figure out if there's trouble ahead, use the Ear Amp. The GPF's Ear Amp looks like a kidney bean but is one of the most sophisticated hearing devices in the world. Just hook it onto your ear and you can hear conversations from afar or through walls. No battery required.

 **Tornado:** Acting like a catapult, the GPF's Tornado is the ideal gadget for catching up to three villains on the run. Just select the number of ropes required and pull the trigger. With the force of a tornado, the ropes will be flung out, wrapping up your enemies within seconds.

Rock Corer:

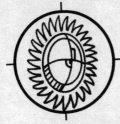

For any secret agent working underground, the Rock Corer is essential. Just pick up this circular saw and twist it, so that its teeth open to the size that you want. Carefully place it against the rock and pull the small lever on its side. Within minutes, it will have created a tunnel for crawling through or a hole for getting much-needed air.

Encryption Notebook:

When you need to keep your notes top-secret, use the GPF's Encryption Notebook (EN). It looks like an ordinary handheld device, but it can change what you write into complete gibberish. Touch the panel marked 'encrypt'.

NOTE: Thumbprint identification is necessary for EN activation. Please make sure yours has been registered at GPF HQ before using for the first time.

Chapter 1:
The Magic Break

It was a rainy day on 9 May and Jack Stalwart was sitting at his desk in his bedroom doing his homework. His Year 5 class was studying the history of the British Empire. In front of him was a long list of British kings and queens who had ruled the country since the time of William the Conqueror. He looked at the list and his eyes glazed over.

'There's no way I'm going to memorize these names by tomorrow.' He sighed.

Kings and Queens of Great Britain
(since William the Conqueror)

Normans	Dates
William I (the Conqueror)	1066–1087
William II (Rufus)	1087–1100
Henry I	1100–1135
Stephen	1135–1154
Plantagenets	
Henry II	1154–1189
Richard I (Lionheart)	1189–1199
John (Lackland)	1199–1216
Henry III	1216–1272
Edward I (Longshanks)	1272–1307
Edward II	1307–1327
Edward III	1327–1377
Richard II	1377–1399
Lancaster	
Henry IV	1399–1413
Henry V	1413–1422
Henry VI	1422–1461
York	
Edward IV	1461–1483
Edward V	1483
Richard III	1483–1485
Tudor	
Henry VII	1485–1509
Henry VIII	1509–1547
Edward VI	1547–1553
Mary I	1553–1558
Elizabeth I	1558–1603
Stuart	
James I	1603–1625
Charles I	1625–1649
The Commonwealth	1649–1660
Charles II	1660–1685
James II	1685–1688
William III and Mary II	1689–1702
Anne	1702–1714
Hanover	
George I	1714–1727
George II	1727–1760
George III	1760–1820
George IV	1820–1830
William IV	1830–1837
Victoria	1837–1901
Saxe-Coburg-Gotha	
Edward VII	1901–1910
Windsor	
George V	1910–1936
Edward VIII	1936
George VI	1936–1952
Elizabeth II	1952–

'There are too many of them.' Jack closed the book and decided to take a break.

He walked over to his bedside table and opened the top drawer. Inside was one of his favourite books: *Master the Art of Magic*. He pulled it out, sat on his bed and began to read the section called 'Appearing Coin' on page thirty-one. Jack smiled to himself. This was much more fun than homework.

Ever since Jack's Uncle Richard had taken him to see the master magician, Ivan the Incredible, in London, he'd been fascinated by the art of illusion. He'd watched as the magician made an enormous elephant disappear right on stage. Towards the end of the show, he'd escaped from a straitjacket while hanging over a fiery pit. 'Incredible' was the right word. Jack had never seen anything like it before.

As soon as he got home that night, Jack had asked his mum for a book on magic. On his birthday, she surprised him with *Master the Art of Magic*. It was the biggest-selling book on magic and, in Jack's opinion, just about the best. Every page was chock-full of exciting tips on how to fool your friends and family with magical tricks. Last night, he had learned how to bend a spoon. Tonight, he was going to learn how to pull a coin out of thin air.

Jack reached into his top drawer and grabbed some sticky tape. Then he pulled a coin out of his trouser pocket. Cutting off a piece of tape, he stuck the coin onto the back of his first finger. Doing as the book said, he reached behind his ear and then flipped his middle finger forward. The coin magically appeared in the palm of his hand.

'Fantastic!' shouted Jack. 'My friends at school are going to love this one!' At that, there was a knock on the door.

'How's the homework going?' said a familiar voice from the other side. It was Jack's mum checking up on his progress.

'Uh, all right, Mum,' said Jack, putting the coin in his pocket and racing back to his desk.

'That's great, honey,' his mum said through the door. 'Don't forget to clean your teeth before you go to bed.'

'OK, Mum,' said Jack. He hoped his mum wouldn't ask to come in.

She didn't, and when he was sure that she'd made her way back downstairs, Jack pulled the coin out of his trouser pocket. 'Now,' he said, 'let's practise that trick again.'

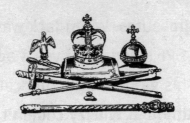

Chapter 2:
The Land of Kings
and Queens

At that moment, Jack's miniature globe began to spin on top of his bedside table. Hearing this, Jack put his magic book away. There were more important things to concentrate on now. It was 7:30 p.m.

Jack was a Secret Agent for the Global Protection Force. The Global Protection Force, or GPF, was a worldwide group of young secret agents determined to fight crime and protect the world's most precious treasures. When Jack was sworn in by the GPF a couple of years ago, he chose as his globe a little one called Whizzy. Although Whizzy couldn't talk, he could give Jack clues about his next mission by spitting jigsaw pieces from his mouth. Since it was precisely 7:30 p.m., that's exactly what Whizzy was going to do.

Whizzy coughed: 'Ahem!' A small jigsaw piece flew out of his mouth and across the room. It bounced off the wall and landed on the floor. Jack bent over and looked to see whether he recognized the shape of the country.

'No way,' said Jack. 'I can't believe it!' he added, looking at its unmistakable shape. 'That's where I live.'

Jack raced to the Magic Map on his bedroom wall. It was a brilliant map of the world, with every country in bright colours. Jack placed the jigsaw piece exactly where he knew it belonged and watched as the name 'Great Britain' appeared on the map.

From inside the country, a red light began to glow. Jack pulled his Book Bag out from under his bed, and checked his Watch Phone for the code of the day. After receiving it, he punched the word – Q-U-E-E-N – into the bag's lock. Almost instantly, it opened, revealing what was tucked inside.

In addition to the usual gadgets, there was the Encryption Notebook, the Ear Amp and the Tornado. The GPF had just added the Heli-Spacer, a device that enabled you to fly using your hands to control your direction. Although Jack hadn't needed it yet, he was hoping he'd get a chance to use it on this mission.

Jack closed his Book Bag and ran over to the map. As the light from inside the country grew to fill his room, he smiled and yelled, 'Off to Great Britain!'

With those words, the red light burst,
swallowing him into the Magic Map.

Chapter 3:
The Tower of Infamy

As soon as Jack arrived, he was aware of something sinister above him. He quickly hit the ground, rolled over twice and got himself out of harm's way. Looking up, Jack noticed a row of iron spikes hanging inside a rounded arch.

'Don't worry,' said a male voice from behind him. 'The only way that portcullis comes down is if I let it down.' Jack knew that the word 'portcullis' meant a gate or grating that slid up and down.

Jack whipped round. Standing nearby

was a man dressed in a long blue jacket with a red crown and two letters – E and R – embroidered on its chest. He also had a red and gold badge attached to his arm. Because of the way he was dressed, Jack knew not only *what* the man was but also *where* he was. The man was a Yeoman Warder, a legendary protector of the Tower of London.

'You must be Jack,' he said. 'The GPF said they'd be sending you. My name is Tommy,' he added. 'I'm one of the Yeoman Warders.'

Jack took a good look at Tommy – the GPF trained him to look at details. He was middle-aged, of average build and had grey hairs sprouting within his brown beard.

'Nice to meet you,' said Jack, excited to be speaking to a real Yeoman Warder. He was fascinated by the history of the Tower of London and had been there several times with his mum and dad. He knew that Yeoman Warders were sometimes called 'Beefeaters' because in the old days they were probably paid their wages in beef.

Jack looked past Tommy to the cobblestone street ahead. Because he'd been here before, he knew that the Tower of London was a popular tourist attraction. Hundreds of tourists usually filled the streets. Today, however, there was no one around.

'What's wrong?' asked Jack, figuring something bad must have happened if there weren't any visitors.

'Well,' said Tommy, taking off his hat and scratching his bald head. 'We have a slight problem.' Before Jack could respond, he added, 'Someone has stolen the Crown Jewels. And between you and me' – he leaned towards Jack – 'the Queen's not pleased.'

Chapter 4:
The Caper

'What?' said Jack, who was completely shocked. 'I can't believe someone's stolen the Crown Jewels!'

'Neither can I,' said Tommy, his face looking serious.

'Have you contacted Scotland Yard or MI5?' asked Jack, referring to the country's finest law-enforcement agencies.

'Not yet,' he said. 'The Queen's given the Warders four hours to locate the crooks before she notifies them herself.'

'How could this have happened?' asked Jack.

'I don't know,' said Tommy. 'It's very embarrassing. The Jewel House is locked up tighter than you would believe. We have some pretty hi-tech security equipment in there,' he added. 'The jewels were there one second and gone the next. We've even looked at the footage from the security cameras.'

'What did you see?' said Jack, anxious to know whether there were any clues on the tapes.

'There were six people viewing the jewels at that time,' explained Tommy. 'Out of nowhere, the lights went out, which meant our cameras couldn't pick up a thing. When they came back on, the same six people were there, looking stunned. We've searched them,' he went on, 'and none of them have the jewels. We've asked them to wait for further questioning in the Jewel House.'

'What about the other tourists in the grounds?' Jack asked.

'We've searched them too and found nothing. Because of that,' Tommy said, 'we've had to let them go. Believe me, this one's a head-scratcher, which is why we called the GPF. We need your help to solve the crime.'

'Which one of the jewels was taken?' asked Jack, knowing that the Crown Jewels were made up of many crowns, orbs and sceptres.

'The Imperial State Crown, the Sovereign's Orb *and* the Sovereign's Sceptre with Cross,' said Tommy.

'No way!' said Jack. Given the value and importance of what was stolen, he

knew this was going to be a special case. The Sovereign's Sceptre with Cross contained the finest cut diamond in the world, the Cullinan I.

'Why don't I take you over to the Jewel House?' offered Tommy. 'The six people who were in there at the time of the theft are being held there. Maybe you can speak to them and get something out of them. Frankly,' he added, 'I'm not sure

they had anything to do with this.'

Tommy led Jack up Water Lane and past the Medieval Palace, St Thomas's Tower and Traitors' Gate. They hung a left at the Wakefield Tower and walked under a stone archway. As they climbed another cobblestone street, Jack spied some black cages through a crumbling stone wall on his right.

'That's where the ravens are,' said Jack, pointing in the direction of the gaps. He remembered seeing them on his last visit. 'Is it true that if one of them leaves, it means that there will be no more kings and queens of Great Britain?'

'That's what they say, young man,' said Tommy. 'I'm not sure I entirely believe it. But, just in case, we clip their wings so that there's no chance of finding out.

Chapter 5:
The Interrogation

Tommy led Jack past a large building with four turrets. This was the White Tower – the oldest part of the Tower of London. It was built after William the Conqueror captured London in 1066. Jack climbed a few stairs to the top of the courtyard. To his left was a paved area with a monument in the middle.

'That's Tower Green,' said Tommy, nodding in the direction of the monument. 'That marks the place where seven famous people were beheaded.'

'Like Anne Boleyn,' said Jack, who'd remembered that Henry VIII had executed his second wife here.

'And Catherine Howard,' added Tommy, naming another of Henry's wives. 'Lord Hastings was beheaded here too.'

Jack gulped at the thought of what it would feel like to have your head chopped off by an axe. He and Tommy hurried past Tower Green and towards a large golden-coloured building that was newer than the others.

'Here we are,' said Tommy, pointing to the building. 'This is Waterloo Barracks. Inside is the Jewel House.' He motioned for Jack to follow him.

Beyond the doorway was a series of rooms with giant cinema screens, each one playing a film about the history of the Queen's jewels. Walking through, they reached an open vault door which led to where the Crown Jewels were kept.

In the middle of the room were five glass cases standing in a row. Each one was as tall as a man and was capped with steel on the top and stone at the

bottom. On either side of the cases was a flat, moving walkway. A clever way, Jack reckoned, to keep the tourists moving through. Because of the theft, the walkway was now turned off.

Jack walked over and looked closely at the cases. The Imperial State Crown was missing from one, while the Sovereign's Sceptre with Cross and the Sovereign's Orb were missing from others. The glass around the case wasn't broken and, as far

as Jack could tell, the top and bottom were still intact. The only thing left was the red and gold pillow on which the jewels once lay.

In the corner of the room were the six people who had been present at the time of the crime. There was a church vicar and a younger man, a mother and her daughter, and an elderly couple. The elderly woman was standing with the help of a walking stick.

Based on first impressions, Jack was going to have to agree with Tommy. They didn't look like a bunch of criminals. More importantly none of them looked as if they were carrying the Crown Jewels.

Jack opened his Book Bag and grabbed his Encryption Notebook. As soon as he placed his thumb over the glass, the Encryption Notebook turned itself on, read his thumbprint and identified him as the rightful owner. Jack detached the pen from the side of the gadget and made a note of the date: 9 May.

When he was ready, he approached the vicar and the young man.

'Hi there,' said Jack. 'My name is Jack Stalwart.' He turned to the vicar first. 'Can I have your name?' he asked.

'Father Type,' he answered, smiling.

Jack turned to the younger man. 'And

yours?' he asked.

'Edward Pigeon,' he replied.

'Thanks,' said Jack, making a few notes on their appearance. Father Type, in particular, had a familiar look about him.

'Would you mind stepping over here while I ask you a few more questions?' He wanted to make sure that they had some privacy, and led the men over to a side room where the Queen's priceless coronation robe hung in a massive glass case.

'Where do you work?' Jack asked, carrying on with the interrogation.

'We both work just off of Tooley Street,' said the vicar.

Jack thought about churches near Tooley Street in London. 'At Southwark Cathedral?' he asked, remembering the location of that famous church.

'Yes, that's right,' said Father Type, nodding. 'At Southwark Cathedral.'

'I was wondering,' said Jack, turning to the vicar first, 'if you could describe exactly what you saw.'

'Nothing significant, my child,' replied Father Type. 'We were on the walkway like everyone else,' he explained, 'adoring the Queen's precious jewels. All of a sudden, the lights went out and when they came back on, the jewels were gone. It gave me quite a fright, really,' he added, shaking his head.

Jack turned to Edward Pigeon. 'Did you see the same thing as Father Type?' he asked the young man.

'Yes,' said Edward. 'Pity really – I only saw the jewels for a few seconds before they vanished.'

Jack thanked both men for their time and called the mother and daughter over. He introduced himself, took their details and asked whether they had noticed anything important.

'Well,' said the mother, 'I do remember hearing something when the lights went

out. It sounded as though someone was whispering something.'

'Do you remember whether it was a man or a woman?' asked Jack.

'It was a man, I think,' she answered, 'although the voice was a bit high-pitched. So I suppose it could have been either.'

'And what about you?' said Jack, turning to the young girl. 'What do you remember?'

'Nothing,' said the girl. She hid herself in her mother's skirt.

Thinking he'd got all he was going to get out of these two, Jack called the elderly couple over.

'Hi there,' he said. He introduced himself and noted down both their names and their contact details. 'Can you tell me whether you saw or heard anything significant before the Crown Jewels went missing?'

'I didn't hear anything, but I certainly smelled something,' said the man.

This was interesting, thought Jack. He made a note of it in his Notebook.

'What did it smell like?' he asked.

'Something sweet,' said the woman. 'Kind of like berries.'

'Is there anything else you can remember?' asked Jack.

'Nothing,' said the man. The woman agreed.

Jack looked at his Notebook and reviewed the information he'd gathered so far on his suspects:

Father Type and Edward Pigeon
(Southwark Cathedral, London)

Nancy and Polly Sommerville
(Brighton, East Sussex)

Ned and Phyllis Royale
(Alton, Hampshire)

He then made a note of the sequence
of events:

Tourists on walkway
Lights go out
Sound of whispering
Smell of something sweet

After securing what Jack thought was
enough information about the suspects,
he and Tommy let them leave the Tower of
London.

'What did I tell you, Jack?' said Tommy, turning to him. 'It's a head-scratcher, isn't it?'

'Sure is,' said Jack. There were no obvious suspects and no obvious means by which the jewels had been stolen.

Tommy looked at his watch, and then looked at Jack. 'We need to find the crooks soon,' he said. 'With three hours left, we're running out of time.'

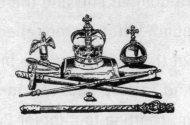

Chapter 6:
The Scam

Jack looked at his Encryption Notebook again and reviewed his notes. *Smell of something sweet, probably ladies perfume. Sound of man or woman whispering in the dark.* He sniffed the air. He didn't smell anything sweet. He listened closely. He couldn't hear anything unusual.

He walked over to the cases again and looked inside. Jack could tell from the indentation in the pillow that the crown itself was fairly large. The sceptre was

long with a pointed end and the orb was
big and round. Whoever took them would
need to put them in something big.

Jack found Tommy, who was in the
other room, chatting to another Beefeater.
Tommy introduced the other man as
Charles.

'Pleased to meet you, Charles,' said Jack. 'I'm trying to narrow down all the different ways someone could have taken the jewels out of their cases,' he explained. 'Could someone have taken them from above?' Jack was thinking that perhaps the tops had been dismantled ahead of time and lifted off without anyone knowing it.

'Nope,' said Charles. 'Not possible. Every morning and night the case is checked from top to bottom to make sure it's intact. Besides,' he added, 'it's made of impenetrable steel. It would be almost impossible to cut through it anyway.'

'What about from below?' asked Jack, who was running out of options. If it wasn't from the top or the sides, then it had to be from underneath.

'No chance there either,' said Tommy. 'Each jewel sits on a pillow which then

sits on a stand. The stand is a moveable
platform that travels down to the Jewel
Master's quarters on the lower ground
level. Once there, the Jewel Master takes
off the jewel, cleans it and then places it
back on the pillow. He then returns it up
to the case.

'You see,' he continued, 'no one but
the Jewel Master has access to the jewels.
The only way to lower and raise that
platform is if you have an access code.
And only the Jewel Master knows it. And
before you think that he's had anything to

do with this, consider that he's nearly eighty years old and has worked here for over fifty-five years. Besides,' he added, 'he's on holiday with his daughter in Greece and the room is under surveillance. We've checked that camera too.'

'Well, if someone were going to steal the Crown Jewels, how would they do it?' asked Jack.

'You got me,' said Charles. 'It would take a miracle. The only time anyone's been able to pull off a stunt like this was on the ninth of May 1671. Colonel Blood was his name,' he said, 'and he did it by dressing up like a vicar. He brought along a pal named Thomas Parrot and the two of them made off with the jewels before being caught—' Charles stopped himself as soon as he realized what he'd said.

Jack was stunned. He couldn't believe

his ears. He'd been fooled. They'd all been fooled! He looked through his Notebook once again. The name the priest had given him was Father Type. Blood has different groups like Type A and Type B. His young assistant was Edward Pigeon – which was very similar to Thomas Parrot!

The two men were playing games with Jack from the start. He stamped his feet on the ground and growled in frustration. Father Type and Thomas Pigeon had pulled off the unimaginable. They had stolen the Crown Jewels and Jack, Tommy and Charles had unknowingly let them escape.

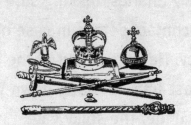

Chapter 7:
The Discovery

But who were these guys and where were the jewels? The men definitely didn't have them when they left.

Jack looked down at the Encryption Notebook. Father Type and Edward Pigeon had said they worked at Southwark Cathedral. Deciding that was as good a place to start as any, Jack pulled out his map of London. Southwark Cathedral wasn't far away.

Pressing the 'encrypt' button on his Notebook, Jack said a quick goodbye to

Tommy and Charles, making sure he had Tommy's contact details in case of an emergency. He hurried out of the Jewel House, past Traitors' Gate, down Water Lane and under the spiky gate.

Once outside the Tower, he jumped on a massive red double-decker bus and found a seat on the upper deck. Jack figured the view from there was as good as any. As the bus lurched forward and began to move through the streets of London, he kept his eyes open for Father Type, Edward Pigeon or any other clue that might help solve the crime.

The bus chugged across Tower Bridge and over to the other side of the River Thames, which was one of the biggest rivers in England. As they drove along Tooley Street, Jack could see Southwark Cathedral straight ahead. It was a beautiful church with a small garden at

the front where visitors could stop and
have a drink or an ice cream. Jack hopped
off the bus and walked briskly towards it.

He entered the church and looked around.

To his left was what Jack had been hoping for – a notice board. He walked over and scanned through the pictures of the clergy. Unfortunately – but unsurprisingly – there wasn't a picture of anyone resembling Father Type. He looked for one like Edward Pigeon. Nothing there either.

Jack exited the church and paused outside. He thought back to his conversation with the two men. Father Type had said that they worked 'off Tooley Street' which Jack took to mean Southwark Cathedral. It was the closest church to that street that he could think of. A basic mistake, he thought. He had given the criminal an answer he could use; he should have let the man provide the information himself.

Although they obviously had nothing to

do with the church, maybe the two men really did work off Tooley Street. Making tracks, Jack left the church garden and headed for that road. Once on it, he could see a sign for one of London's most popular attractions, the London Dungeon.

He stopped and looked at the advert for the Dungeon's latest exhibits: EXPERIENCE THE GREAT PLAGUE! WITNESS THE GREAT FIRE OF LONDON! Although it was an unlikely place to find these men, Jack bought a ticket and went inside. He quickly looked around and when he was satisfied there was no sign of them, left the Dungeon and carried on.

Soon he saw a poster advertising a show at the Magic Theatre. He remembered this place from when he came to see Ivan the Incredible with his Uncle Richard. He approached a poster listing all the performances.

Ivan the Incredible! The greatest illusionist of all time . . . Witness him escape from a fiery pit! Watch an elephant disappear before your very eyes! Book now, or miss out. Last show, tonight 5:00 p.m.

In the lower right-hand corner of the poster was a picture of Ivan the Incredible and his assistant dressed in their costumes from the show. Jack leaned closer to have a look. Underneath the costumes, their wigs and their beards, Jack noticed something familiar.

Now everything made sense. The lights going out, the sweet smell of berries, the chanting and the cleverly faked names – all these were tactics magicians used to distract their audiences. Yes, Jack thought, there was no doubt. Father Type was Ivan the Incredible and Edward Pigeon his loyal assistant, Jazz.

Chapter 8:
The Preparation

But why would Ivan and Jazz want to steal the Crown Jewels in the first place? Weren't they worried that someone like Jack would recognize them? Perhaps, Jack figured, for a showman like Ivan a crime wasn't worth committing if it wasn't done in front of an 'audience'.

Jack looked at his watch. It was 4:00 p.m. He needed to think of a plan before Ivan the Incredible's last show started at 5:00 p.m. Jack knew that if he didn't catch him tonight, the jewels would probably be lost for ever.

He ducked into a nearby café and ordered a smoothie. He pulled out his Encryption Notebook, set it back to normal and made a list of what he remembered of Ivan's last show. He marked an 'X' beside the trick where he planned to spring his trap. If everything went according to plan, Jack would have an easy time bringing this magic madman to justice.

Double-checking the contents of his Book Bag, he took a sip of his drink and looked at his Watch Phone. It was 4:30 p.m. There was only half an hour to buy a ticket and get to his seat, ready for the show.

Jack hurried to the ticket office, bought a ticket near the stage and went inside. By the time he'd found his seat, there were five minutes to go. The lights were starting to flicker – the show was about to begin.

A man's voice came over the loud speaker:

'Ladies and gentlemen, welcome to the Magic Theatre. Tonight, you will be treated to a performance by one of the greatest magicians of all time – Ivan the Incredible! As tonight is his last performance, put your hands together to give him a warm welcome.'

The audience around Jack erupted with wild applause.

Yes, thought Jack, I've got a very warm welcome for you indeed.

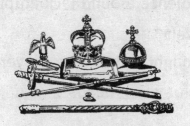

Chapter 9:
The Show

Almost as soon as the curtains opened, an incredible flash of light burst from the centre of the stage and turned into a towering wall of flames. Jack was startled. He didn't remember this part of the show. He put his right hand over his eyes to shield them from the heat.

Carefully, he peeked through his fingers and spied Ivan the Incredible walking through the fire. Ivan emerged from the flames and stepped unharmed to the front of the stage towards his screaming fans. Although Ivan was a crook, Jack couldn't help but be impressed.

Ivan the Incredible lifted his arms to the audience, as if he were begging for applause. The dutiful spectators did just what he asked. They broke into such a roar of claps and cheers that Jack could barely think.

'Welcome! Welcome!' Ivan called to the audience. 'So glad you could be here for my very last show! Tonight,' he said, 'is a very special night. It's special for two reasons. The first is that I have created a brand-new show just for you. Its theme is "Kings and Queens", in honour of this great country.

'The second,' Ivan the Incredible continued, 'is because an old friend of mine is sitting in the audience tonight.' He looked down at Jack as a spotlight was directed on top of him. 'His name is Jack

Stalwart, and if you give him some
encouragement, maybe he will join me on
stage later tonight.'

The audience whistled and cheered for

Jack, who slumped down in his chair, trying not to be noticed.

How did he know I was here? he asked himself. Although Jack was sitting close to the stage, the lights had been out until Ivan had burst through the flames. This is terrible, thought Jack. Not only had Ivan changed the show, he'd ruined Jack's chances of making an arrest without causing a big fuss.

The crowd started chanting again: 'Ivan . . . Ivan . . . Ivan . . .'

Ivan the Incredible looked at Jack and smiled before turning back towards the soaring flames. He walked through them again, but this time, as he did so, the fire vanished, taking Ivan with it. Jack sat bolt upright in his chair. He wondered whether Ivan had left the show for good.

Within seconds, a beautiful white bird flew down from the rafters and onto the stage. Jack took a deep breath and settled back into this seat. This was one of Ivan's tricks. He hadn't left the show yet.

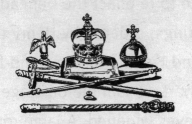

Chapter 10:
The Lure

Almost as soon as the bird landed, it became Ivan the Incredible again. But this time, he was dressed like Henry VIII, who was King of England in the early 1500s.

From the right side of the stage, Jack could hear a noise. It sounded as if someone was pushing something heavy on rollers.

'Ladies and gentlemen!' said Ivan. 'As promised, I have themed this show around the great kings and queens of Britain. For my first feat of illusion, I would like to re-enact the beheading of Lord Hastings, ordered by Henry the Eighth. And I would like my kind friend, Jack Stalwart, to join me on stage.'

Jack's eyes widened. A large round block of wood was being rolled onto the stage by Ivan's assistant, Jazz. It looked like a tree stump. Stuck in the middle was a shiny, sharp axe with its handle pointing straight up in the air. Jack sat frozen in his seat. He gulped and looked around. He could hear the audience starting to chant his name. 'Jack . . . Jack . . . Jack . . .'

He looked up at Ivan the Incredible, who was smiling and motioning for Jack to come on stage.

Jack didn't know what to do. He knew that magic was all about 'illusion'. He knew that Ivan the Incredible wouldn't or couldn't actually behead him on stage.

But then again, this wasn't an ordinary
evening. Ivan was trying to get away with
a terrible crime and Jack was the only
person standing in his way.

'No thanks,' Jack shouted to Ivan.

'Did you hear that, audience?' yelled Ivan. 'He's a bit nervous. Why don't we give Jack some encouragement?' He lifted his arms and waved his hands at the throngs of men, women and children in the theatre.

The audience's chants grew louder. They were cheering for Jack. Above the noise, he heard a man from two rows back.

'Come on, kid!' the man shouted. 'It's just a magic trick!' He's right, Jack told himself, trying to stay calm. It is just a magic trick. There was no way Ivan could hurt Jack in front of all these people. Besides, getting on stage might give Jack a chance to figure out where the Crown Jewels actually were.

'All right! All right!' said Jack as he grabbed his Book Bag and made his way on stage.

Chapter 11:
The Axe

'So wonderful to see you again,' said Ivan to Jack as he placed his hand on Jack's back. Ivan led him towards Jazz, who was waiting next to the wooden block. The audience was chanting in the background.

'I know you took the jewels,' said Jack, looking up at Ivan. 'Why don't you just tell me where they are and we can forget about the whole thing?'

'I don't know what you're talking about,' Ivan said, smiling. 'I don't see any jewels around here.' He shoved Jack towards Jazz and turned back to his adoring audience.

'Ladies and gentleman,' said Ivan, assuming the role of Henry VIII. 'The person before you is a traitor!' He turned round and pointed to Jack. 'He has committed the crime of high treason and is therefore sentenced to death by beheading.'

While Ivan was talking to his audience, Jazz pulled the axe out of the wood. He motioned for Jack to put his neck in place. Jack knelt down before the block, looking at the deep cut where the axe had been. There was no doubt something sharp had made that cut. He just hoped for his sake it wasn't this axe. Jack reluctantly lowered his head.

'Ladies and gentlemen!' said Ivan as Henry VIII. 'The beheading of Lord Hastings!'

Quickly, Jack closed his eyes. In the background he could hear Jazz pick up the axe and swing it into the air before letting it come down over Jack's neck.

He was aware of a funny feeling on his neck and then felt something warm dripping over his ears.

Slowly, he opened his eyes and lifted his head. To his relief and amazement the rest of his body came with it. Jazz hadn't cut his head off after all and the warm feeling was just fake blood that had oozed out of the magic axe.

The theatre was filled with applause. This time, the cheers weren't just for Ivan and Jazz. They were for Jack too. As Jack started to move off stage, Jazz came up behind him.

'Leave us alone,' he said, grabbing Jack's left arm tightly, 'or we'll kill you for real.'

Chapter 12:
The Revelation

Tired from nearly having his head chopped off, Jack made his way off the stage and back to his seat. Ivan the Incredible left the stage briefly and came back dressed as a different king before he spoke to the audience.

'Now we are fast-forwarding our journey through the kings and queens of the past to Charles the Second. Charles the Second, as many of you will know, was King during the Great Plague of 1665 and the Great Fire of London in 1666. He also made two of the three Crown Jewels that the Queen uses today.'

That fact made Jack's ears prick up. He wondered where Ivan was going with this 'act' and whether there was going to be some sort of clue that would lead Jack to where the jewels were being kept. He listened carefully to what Ivan the Incredible had to say.

'King Charles the Second created this beautiful orb,' said Ivan. At the mention of the orb, Ivan lifted his left hand. From nowhere, a bubble appeared above his hand with an image of the orb sitting in a glass case. Jack rubbed his eyes, as did the girl sitting next to him.

'He also created this beautiful sceptre,' added Ivan as he conjured another image into the air, this time of the sceptre inside its glass case. 'Sitting at the top of the sceptre,' he explained, 'is the First Star of Africa, also known as the Cullinan I, the largest cut diamond in the world!

'Finally,' he said, 'the third and final treasure was not created by Charles the Second, but by George the Sixth in 1937.'

POOF!

At the mention of this new king's name, Ivan's costume changed to that of George VI.

'The Imperial State Crown was made in 1937,' continued Ivan. 'Some say it's the most beautiful piece in the entire collection. There are over 2,800 diamonds and 270 pearls.' With a wave of his hand, he created a third image in the air, one of the Imperial State Crown, also in a glass case.

Looking at the images, Jack had a horrible idea. What if the jewels really were still in their cases, just as Ivan was showing them? Jack had been baffled by

how Ivan and Jazz had escaped with the jewels from the Tower; they were so big. But perhaps, Jack thought, they never did. Maybe the jewels were still in the Jewel House. Maybe Ivan and Jazz had created an illusion to make Jack and Tommy think the jewels had been stolen, so they could actually steal them another time.

'Yes, ladies and gentlemen,' said Ivan, causing Jack to snap out of his thoughts, 'this is our last glimpse into the world of the kings and queens. Our journey ends here with a lasting image for all of you of the jewels that we have stolen tonight.' Ivan paused and then added, 'We bid you farewell!' Then the two men disappeared in a puff of smoke before Jack had time to register what they had said.

Chapter 13:
The Mad Dash

Jack was stunned. Like the rest of the audience, he was trying to work out whether this was a trick or if what Ivan had said was true. As the audience was whispering, Jack hurried onto the stage. Ducking in and out of the wings, he looked for any sign of Ivan and Jazz. But they had completely disappeared.

Jack returned to the spot where they had been standing. Wondering if they'd used a trap door, he looked down. Sure enough, there was a small copper ring. He bent down and pulled it hard. A thin rectangular door flew open. He lowered himself through the hole and climbed down a flight of narrow steps. As soon as he reached the lower level, he started running. In the distance he could hear Ivan and Jazz.

'Quick!' said one of the men.

'He's coming!' said the other.

BANG!

It sounded like a door. Jack ran as fast as he could, down a long hall and towards the sounds of the men. As he ran, he passed photos of Ivan and Jazz in various poses and outfits. When he reached a steel door, he flung it open.

BLAM!

In front of Jack was the Magic Theatre car park. It was full to the brim of parked cars. So many, in fact, that it was an absolute jam. There's no way that Ivan and Jazz can get themselves out of this, thought Jack.

BBRRRMMM!

In the distance a motorcycle engine revved up. Jack looked in the direction of the noise and saw Ivan and Jazz speeding down the road on a red Ducati.

'Drat!' said Jack, frustrated they'd escaped by bike. I have to warn Tommy, he said to himself as he dialled Tommy's number on his Watch Phone. But there was no answer.

Working quickly, Jack knelt down. He unzipped his Book Bag and pulled out a miniature disc. Placing his hands on the outside of the disc, he slid them around until the disc grew larger. He then grabbed a small steel rod and pulled it three times until it grew to be taller than him.

Plunging the rod into a small hole at the edge of the disc, Jack pushed the button marked 'Prop' on his Watch Phone. Instantly, two propellers shot out of the rod and began to spin. This was the GPF's Heli-Spacer – Jack's only hope for getting to the Tower on time.

He hopped on and clipped the Heli-

Spacer's belt around himself. Then he raised his hands in the air. The Heli-Spacer began to rise. All Jack needed was one good thrust. As he threw his arms forward, the Heli-Spacer took off. Soon Jack was flying over the River Thames in pursuit of Ivan and Jazz.

Chapter 14:
The Groans

Within minutes, Jack was hovering above Tower Green. He slowly dropped his hands to his sides and he was lowered safely to the ground. After touching down, he hopped off, took apart the device and packed it away.

Jack glanced at his Watch Phone. It was 6:30 p.m.

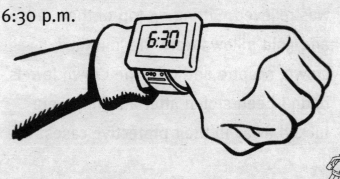

He dialled Tommy's number again, but still there was no answer. He looked across the courtyard and spied Ivan and Jazz. They were making their way to the entrance of the Jewel House. Keeping low, Jack ran towards the doors and pressed his ear against them to listen. There was no sound of Ivan and Jazz. Quickly, he entered the first chamber.

As he moved from room to room, Jack was aware of two things: 1) There was no sign of Ivan and Jazz anywhere; and 2) Tommy and Charles were missing too. None of the other Beefeaters seemed to be around either.

When he reached the last room, Jack was relieved. Sitting on top of their red and gold pillows were the 'missing' crown, sceptre and orb. The Crown Jewels hadn't been stolen after all. They were tucked away in their protective cases. The

illusion that Ivan and Jazz had created
had stopped working.

Then, out of nowhere, Jack heard something strange. It sounded like someone or something groaning. He pulled his Ear Amp out of his pocket and hooked it into the inside of his ear. Although it resembled a tiny kidney bean, the Ear Amp could make even the faintest of sounds seem much louder.

As he listened, Jack could hear the noise more clearly. It was human and it was coming from the floor above. Unfortunately for Jack, there was no obvious way up to the upper level. The only way he could get to the next floor was to slice through the ceiling. He looked a bit closer – it was made of stone.

Figuring the Queen wouldn't mind a little inconvenience like a hole in the ceiling, Jack clambered on top of the orb's case and pulled out his Rock Corer.

The Rock Corer worked a bit like an apple corer, but it could slice a tunnel through hard rock.

Jack set the width to the size of his own body. Strapping on some goggles to protect his eyes, he pulled the cord. Sounding like an electric saw, the Rock Corer began to eat away the stone. Within minutes, Jack had created a hole big

enough to crawl through. He put the
gadget away and heaved himself up to
the next level. In the corner, he could see
Tommy and four other Beefeaters. He
raced over to them and crouched down.

'Are you all right?' Jack asked.

'Uhhhh,' groaned Tommy. He tried to focus his eyes and look at Jack. 'It was the vicar,' he explained. 'He came back after you left. He said something to us,' he added. 'I don't remember anything after that.'

'He hypnotized you,' explained Jack. 'And put you in a trance.'

'Huh?' said Tommy.

'He's not a vicar,' said Jack. 'He's a magician. And he's in the building right now! He's come to steal the Crown Jewels.'

'What?' said Tommy, sounding confused. 'What do you mean? They've already been stolen.'

'Not quite,' said Jack. 'I'll explain later. Are there any secret passages in the barracks?' He wasn't sure how they would have known about them, but he was guessing that Ivan and Jazz had used them to leave the building.

'Yeah,' said Tommy. 'In the first room as you enter the Jewel House there are several wooden panels. Behind the panel with "Elizabeth the Second" on it is a door which leads you downstairs to the Jewel Master's Quarters.'

'Perfect,' said Jack. 'I need to run. Are you going to be OK?' he asked Tommy.

'Of course,' said Tommy. 'Now go and catch those thieves.'

Chapter 15:
The Getaway

Jack left Tommy and carefully lowered himself down on top of the glass case. He sat for a moment, thinking about the jewels in their cases. The only way Ivan and Jazz were going to be able to get to them was from the Jewel Master's Quarters underneath. Jack could use the Rock Corer to get to the lower level, or he could try to head them off at the front door.

WOOMPH!

Jack was startled by a noise. In fact, it wasn't just the sound. The case he was sitting on was starting to shake.

WOOMPH!

It happened again.

Quickly, Jack climbed off the case and onto the ground. Before his eyes, the sceptre and the orb were being lowered down until they had vanished from sight.

WOOMPH!

The sound was coming from the other end of the room now. It was the case with the Imperial State Crown. It was being lowered down too.

'Arrgh!' growled Jack in frustration. Ivan and Jazz were stealing the jewels! There was no time to try to use the secret passage. Jack's only option was to stop them as they left by the front door.

He dashed through the final chamber and towards the first room. Almost as soon as he entered the room with the panels, Ivan and Jazz burst out of the secret passage, crashing into him and sending him backwards onto the floor.

'Better luck next time, kid!' screamed Ivan as he and Jazz raced outside through the arched doorway. Both men were carrying bags on their backs. Sticking out of one of them was the top of the Sceptre with Cross.

Jack had only seconds to recover. His back was hurting, but he didn't have time to think. Ivan and Jazz were getting away and Jack needed to stop them before they

committed a serious crime against the Queen.

Jack pulled himself together and ran after the thieves. Ivan and Jazz were sprinting across the courtyard to the left of the White Tower and under an archway. On the other side of the archway was the River Thames. Jack figured that Ivan and Jazz had a speedboat waiting so that they could make their escape.

Even though he was running as fast as he could, Jack was struggling to catch up with the crooks. Ivan and Jazz were bigger than him and their legs were twice as long. They'd already made it past the archway and were kneeling down next to the wall of the Thames. The only thing that could stop them was the GPF's Tornado. Smiling to himself, Jack pulled it out of his Book Bag and prepared to strike.

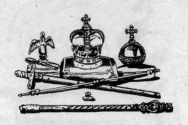

Chapter 16:
The Tornado

As Ivan and Jazz assembled their gear, Jack knelt down on the ground. He lifted the Tornado and set the switch to '2'.

'Ready . . . Aim . . .' said Jack, and he pulled the launcher.

Two ropes shot out of the gadget towards Ivan and Jazz. As soon as they hit their targets, the ropes swirled furiously, again and again. They bound the crooks' feet first and then their hands.

'Noooo!' said Ivan, struggling to break out of its grip.

'Arrghhh!' yelled Jazz as he tried to bite off the rope.

But the power of the Tornado was too strong. Jack watched as the rope continued to wrap Ivan and Jazz up, so that in the end all you could see were their noses and mouths through two tiny windows.

When Jack reached the men, he had to laugh. Ivan and Jazz were so tightly wound that they looked like a pair of sausages.

'Let us go, you brat!' yelled Ivan. Jack could tell it was him by the look in his eyes.

'Sorry, guys,' replied Jack, pleased that he'd foiled one of the greatest magicians of all time. 'I'm afraid you've done this to yourselves. Let's just hope the Queen doesn't decide to chop your heads off.'

As Ivan and Jazz cursed and tried to wriggle free, Jack called Scotland Yard. He figured Tommy wouldn't mind him calling

them now. The caper of the Crown Jewels
had been solved. Within minutes, the
officers arrived and dragged Ivan and Jazz

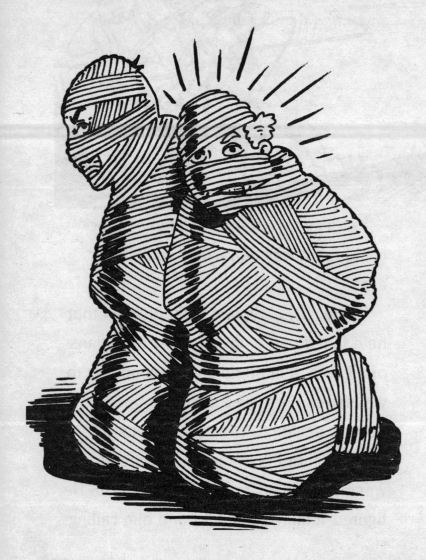

away – since they couldn't walk. Jack reckoned they were probably going away for a very long time, if the Queen had anything to say about it.

Chapter 17:
The Surprise Visitor

As Jack stood there in the Tower grounds, reflecting on his mission, a friendly voice came from behind.

'Well done, son.' It was Tommy. He was obviously feeling better. 'I don't know how we can thank you enough,' he said, putting out his hand to shake Jack's.

'It was nothing,' said Jack. 'It's my job.'

Just then, he saw two black limousines driving smoothly but quickly through the Tower grounds.

'Uh-oh,' said Tommy. 'Looks like we've got company.'

Jack watched as Secret Service agents hopped out of the car. They looked around before opening the back passenger door. Somebody important must be inside, Jack thought.

An older woman stepped out of the car. Jack couldn't believe his eyes. It was the Queen of England – Queen Elizabeth II – and she was walking straight towards him.

'So,' she said, with a pleasant smile, 'you must be Jack.'

Jack stared with his mouth open. Tommy bowed to Her Majesty and Jack quickly did the same.

'I cannot thank you enough,' said the Queen. 'You have saved my most precious jewels. You are a very brave boy.'

Jack figured Scotland Yard had contacted her with the news. 'It was nothing, Your Majesty,' he said, shrugging his shoulders.

She looked knowingly at Tommy and smiled. 'If there's anything I can do for you, please do let me know.'

Jack couldn't think of anything he could ask the Queen for, but then he remembered something. 'Well,' he said, 'I kind of need some help with my homework.'

'What kind of homework?' the Queen asked.

'I need to memorize all the kings and queens of Great Britain by tomorrow,' said Jack.

'Let's see what we can do about that,' said the Queen. 'I know a bit about the subject,' she added, smiling again. 'Why don't you come with me and we'll give you a lift.'

Jack turned to Tommy and waved

goodbye. Tommy did the same, and added a wink.

Climbing into the limousine's back seat, Jack sat down opposite the Queen. She began to tell him about the British monarchy. Over the next hour, she taught him everything he needed to know, so that by the time the limousine arrived at his house there was no need to do any more homework.

'Thanks a lot,' said Jack as he stepped out of the car.

'No,' said the Queen, 'thank *you*. I am extremely grateful for all that you've done.'

'Don't mention it, Your Majesty,' Jack replied, and he bowed politely.

The door to the limousine closed and the car pulled away, leaving Jack alone at the front gate to his house. Looking at his Watch Phone, Jack cringed. It was getting on; it was 9:00 p.m.

Even though he figured his parents were asleep, there was no way he wanted to risk entering the house through the front door. If he got caught, he'd have to explain to his mother why he was out so late. After punching a few buttons on his Watch Phone, Jack was transported back to his room. As soon as he arrived, he looked at the clock on his bedside table. It was just after half-past seven.

He took off his Book Bag and hid it

under his bed. Changing into his pyjamas, he brushed his teeth and crawled under the covers. Reaching into his bedside table, he pulled out Master the Art of Magic. Although he didn't like Ivan the Incredible any more, Jack still loved magic.

'Now,' he said as he turned to page thirty-two, 'let's find another trick . . .'